Based on *The Railway Series* by the Rev. W. Awdry

Illustrations by
Robin Davies and Creative Design

EGMONT

EGMONT

We bring stories to life

ISBN 978 1 4052 3475 7

1 3 5 7 9 10 8 6 4 2

Printed in Italy

The Forest Stewardship Council (FSC) is an international, non-governmental organisation dedicated to promoting responsible management of the world's forests. FSC operates a system of forest certification and product labelling that allows consumers to identify wood and wood-based products from well managed forests.

For more information about Egmont's paper buying policy please visit www.egmont.co.uk/ethicalpublishing

For more information about the FSC please visit their website at www.fsc.uk.org

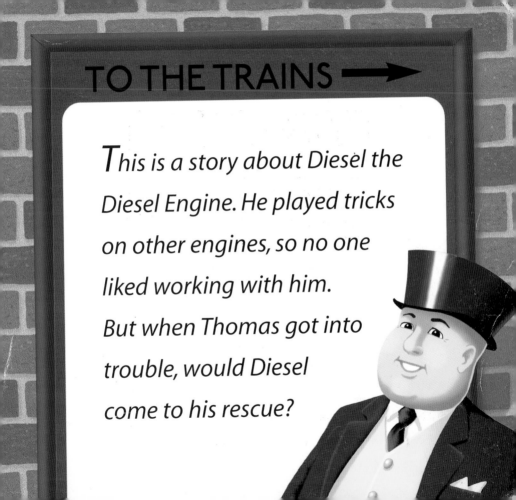

This is a story about Diesel the Diesel Engine. He played tricks on other engines, so no one liked working with him. But when Thomas got into trouble, would Diesel come to his rescue?

One day, Percy wasn't feeling well. His joints ached and he couldn't breathe properly. The Fat Controller came to inspect him.

"You need to go to the Works to be repaired," he said. "I'll have to get another engine to do your work until you're better."

The Fat Controller phoned other Railways to see if anyone could spare an engine. But the only available engine was Diesel.

The Fat Controller didn't want to use Diesel because the last time he had worked at his station, he had caused so much trouble that he had been sent away in disgrace. But, as no other engine could help out, Diesel had to do.

The next day, Diesel came to the station to collect the Troublesome Trucks. Thomas was not happy to see him because Diesel had played so many tricks on him before.

"Take these trucks to the Harbour," Thomas said. "But don't play any silly tricks!" he warned him.

"Yes, Thomas. Of course I won't play tricks. I'll do whatever I'm told," Diesel said, slyly.

The Troublesome Trucks teased Diesel.

"Yes, Thomas. Of course I won't play tricks. I'll do whatever I'm told," they said, in Diesel's voice.

Diesel was angry. "I'll teach you!" he roared and bumped into them roughly, sending them flying into a siding.

The trucks crashed through the buffers and slid off the track.

Diesel hadn't meant the trucks to crash, he had only wanted to scare them. But, he still wanted them to do as they were told, so he said, "That will teach you to laugh at me!"

The Fat Controller was disappointed with Diesel.

"You will go back to the Other Railway as soon as I can arrange it," he said sternly. "I *won't* have trouble on my Railway!"

After such a severe telling-off, Diesel was glad to be going home.

A few days later, Daisy was going up a hill when she felt something splash against her wheels. When she stopped at the next station, she felt hot and her joints were stiff.

"You've lost your oil," her Driver said. "Bertie can take your passengers while we get you repaired."

Thomas had to go over the hill where Daisy had spilt her oil. He was halfway up when his wheels started slipping on the oil.

Suddenly, Thomas, Annie and Clarabel slipped back down the hill. As they reached the bottom, Clarabel's wheels bounced off the main track on to an unfinished siding. Her front wheels fell off the end of the track and sank into the mud. Thomas was left stranded across the main track.

Diesel was at the next station, waiting to go home. He laughed when he heard what had happened, but then he realised Thomas was blocking the track so he couldn't get past.

"Bother!" Diesel said, crossly. "I'll have to help Thomas or I can't get home."

Workmen cleaned the oil off the tracks. Then they put sand on them to help Diesel grip them. Diesel moved slowly forward and was coupled to Thomas. Wooden railway sleepers were put under Clarabel's wheels, so she could be pulled back on to the rails.

"Thank you for coming to help, Diesel," said Thomas. "We could have been stuck here all day!"

Diesel gripped the sanded rails and pulled with all his strength. Slowly and carefully, he pulled Thomas, Annie and Clarabel back on to the main track.

"Well done, Diesel," said Thomas. "You have been a Really Useful Engine!"

Diesel smiled. It felt good to be helpful for a change instead of always causing trouble.

Diesel carefully pulled Thomas, Annie and Clarabel over the slippery hill and on to The Fat Controller's station.

"Good work, Diesel!" said The Fat Controller. "You've been so helpful today that I am happy for you to come back to work at my station!"

Diesel smiled. He was pleased that he was going home, but he was also glad that he could come back again to work for The Fat Controller!

The Thomas Story Library is THE definitive collection of stories about Thomas and ALL his friends.

5 more Thomas Story Library titles will be chuffing into your local bookshop in August 2008!

Jeremy
Hector
BoCo
Billy
Whiff

And there are even more Thomas Story Library books to follow later

So go on, start your Thomas Story Library NOW!

A Fantastic Offer for Thomas the Tank Engine Fans!

STICK POUND COIN HERE

In every Thomas Story Library book like this one, you will find a special token. Collect 6 Thomas tokens and we will send you a brilliant Thomas poster, and a double-sided bedroom door hanger! Simply tape a £1 coin in the space above, and fill out the form overleaf.

TO BE COMPLETED BY AN ADULT

To apply for this great offer, ask an adult to complete the coupon below
and send it with a pound coin and 6 tokens, to:
THOMAS OFFERS, PO BOX 715, HORSHAM RH12 5WG

☐ Please send a Thomas poster and door hanger. I enclose 6 tokens
plus a £1 coin. (Price includes P&P)

Fan's name...

Address...

....Postcode.............................

Date of birth..

Name of parent/guardian...

Signature of parent/guardian..

Please allow 28 days for delivery. Offer is only available while stocks last. We reserve the right to change
the terms of this offer at any time and we offer a 14 day money back guarantee. This does not affect your
statutory rights.

☐ Data Protection Act: If you do not wish to receive other similar offers from us or companies we
recommend, please tick this box. Offers apply to UK only.